CYCLE OF

REVELATION

By

Christopher McCarty

Dedication

To a great friend Scott Reed.

No chance this book would have been completed without his unwavering help and loyalty.

Thank you.

Acknowledgments

I would appreciate an oriented to show my unwavering gratitude to my wife. Though we are separated now, I wouldn't even be here, let alone have completed these projects without her standing by my side, while bed ridden for almost a year after a work accident leaving me with two broken legs.

We may have had our disagreements, but I will always love you for helping me in the most vulnerable time of my adult life.

I appreciate you more than you'll ever know.

Author Biography

Christopher McCarty, born April 28, 1982, in Bakersfield, California, is a carpenter with over 20 years of experience working for Don Kinzel Construction. He has built schools, hospitals, and public service buildings, all while reflecting on complex ideas that have shaped his writing.

An avid fisherman with a deep connection to the Kern River, Christopher explores the river's misunderstood dangers in his work. A work accident in 2022 sparked a spiritual journey that led him to write and explore societal issues, including the militarization of law enforcement and the spiritual aspects of the judicial system.

Christopher is the author of Killing an Agenda and is currently working on two major projects: a guide to custodial detention and a spiritual analysis of court practices through the lens of ancient rituals. He is also launching Anglers Lobby, a business focused on the political side of the fishing industry.

Christopher plans to move to undeveloped forest land, where he will build a home and continue his personal and creative pursuits.

Contact Information

Personal Email: Tophermcbity@gmail.com

Business Email: Thegoods144@exccess.com

Introduction

The Hidden Power of Words and Beliefs

"Language is the road map of a culture. It tells you where its people come from and where they are going."

- Rita Mae Brown

Language is like the glue that holds people together. Throughout history, empires used language to unite their people and spread their influence. For instance, in ancient Mesopotamia, the Akkadian language became the common tongue under the rule of Sargon of Akkad. This unified language allowed people from different regions and backgrounds to communicate effectively. It helped in administration, trade, and cultural exchange. The spread of the Akkadian language made it easier for the rulers to govern their empire and for people to share ideas and knowledge, creating a sense of unity among diverse populations.

Laws, on the contrasting hand, are the rules that keep societies in order. Ancient empires understood that having clear laws helped them maintain control and ensure fairness. The Code of Hammurabi, created by the Babylonian king Hammurabi around 1750 BCE, is one of the earliest examples of written laws. These laws covered various aspects of daily life, such as trade, property, and family matters. By having a set of written laws, Hammurabi's empire could handle disputes and maintain order more effectively. This idea of written laws was later adopted by other empires as well. Spirituality and religion have also been the strong in shaping the empires. Many empires used religion to unite their people and legitimize their rule. For instance, the Ancient Egyptians believed that their pharaohs were gods on Earth, which helped the rulers maintain power and command loyalty. Similarly, the Byzantine Empire used Christianity as a unifying force. Emperor Constantine converted to Christianity and made it the official religion of the empire. This helped to unite the people under a common belief system and strengthened the emperor's authority.

The combination of language, law, and spirituality allowed empires to create a strong sense of identity among their people. These elements worked together to ensure that the empire could function smoothly and maintain control over its vast territories. For example, the Inca Empire in South America used the Quechua language, a legal system called the Inca law, and the worship of their gods to bring together diverse groups of people. This helped them create a strong and unified empire that lasted for centuries.

Over time, the influence of these empires and their use of language, law, and spirituality has shaped the world we live in today. Many modern legal systems, languages, and religious practices have their roots in ancient empires. This shows how important these elements were in creating powerful and lasting societies and they still are shaping and influence the world, we live in.

"Words can be like X-rays if you use them properly — they'll go through anything."

- Aldous Huxley

Words are powerful tools that help us communicate and share ideas. John Steinbeck, a famous writer, understood that words carry great power, but he also knew that their meanings can change over time. For example, the word "gay" used to mean happy and cheerful, but now it is commonly used to describe someone who is attracted to the same gender. This shift in meaning shows how language evolves and adapts to new situations and cultural changes. By understanding the power of words and their shifting meanings, we can better understand the world around us. Many phrases we learn as children have deeper meanings that we may not fully understand at first. Like the phrase, *"Actions Speak Louder Than Words,"* teaches us that what people do is more important than what they say. This means that someone can make promises, but their true character is shown by their actions. Another example is the phrase *"Don't Judge A Book By Its Cover,"* which reminds us not to form opinions about someone or something based solely on appearances. These phrases carry important lessons and the wisdom of centuries in them, and when we understand them, we can easily understand the happenings around us. Someone wisely said that history is like a "touchstone." To really understand what's happening now, we need to look back at the past and compare. This helps us predict what might happen in the future. Throughout history, there have been many examples of how words and phrases have shaped societies and influenced people. In Ancient Greece, philosophers like Socrates and Plato used words to teach and inspire others. Their ideas about ethics, politics, and knowledge have had a lasting impact on Western thought. Similarly, during the American Revolution, powerful speeches like Patrick Henry's "Give me liberty, or give me death!" inspired people to fight for their freedom.

As we grow older, we learn that some phrases have different meanings depending on the context in which they are used. For example, the phrase *"Break a Leg"* is often used to wish someone good luck, especially in the performing arts. While it sounds like it means to hurt yourself, it actually means the opposite. Understanding these different meanings helps us communicate more effectively and appreciate the richness of language. The power of words is also evident in literature and storytelling. Great writers like John Steinbeck and William Shakespeare have used words to create lively images and convey deep emotions. Their stories have the power to take us to different worlds and help us see things from new perspectives. By reading and engaging with literature, we can expand our understanding of language and its potential to shape our thoughts and feelings. There is on deny that words carry immense power, but their meanings can change over time. By understanding the deeper meanings of phrases and the context in which they are used, we can become better communicators and more empathetic individuals. Throughout history, words have inspired change and shaped societies, demonstrating their lasting impact.

"And God said to Noah, 'I have determined to make an end of all flesh, for the earth is filled with violence through them. Behold, I will destroy them with the earth.'"

- Genesis 6:13 (ESV)

Before the Great Flood, the world was a very different place. According to the Bible, people lived much longer, often reaching hundreds of years. This long lifespan allowed them to gather vast amounts of knowledge and wisdom. The descendants of Adam and Eve, like Noah, inherited this wisdom. They were skilled in various crafts, agriculture, and building. However, the Bible also tells us that many people used their knowledge for wicked purposes, leading to widespread corruption and violence. This misuse of wisdom contributed to God's decision to cleanse the earth with the flood. In those ancient times, wisdom was passed down through generations, often through oral traditions. People shared stories, teachings, and practical knowledge with their children and grandchildren. For example, Enoch, a great-grandfather of Noah, was known for his deep understanding of God's ways and his close relationship with the Creator. He walked with God and was taken to heaven without experiencing death. Enoch's wisdom and spiritual insights would have been shared with his descendants, providing guidance and understanding about God's will and the importance of living a righteous life.

The Great Flood was a significant turning point in history. When God decided to flood the earth, He instructed Noah to build an ark and save his family and pairs of every kind of animal. The floodwaters covered the entire earth, wiping out all living creatures except those on the ark. This event resulted in the loss of countless lives and the knowledge they possessed. It is believed that much of the wisdom and understanding from the pre-flood world was lost or erased, as those who perished in the flood took their knowledge with them. After the flood, Noah and his family emerged as the only survivors. They were tasked with repopulating the earth and rebuilding society. With the loss of many wise individuals, the survivors had to rely on their own knowledge and experiences to start anew. This marked the beginning of a new era, where the descendants of Noah would have to rediscover and relearn many of the skills and wisdom that had been lost. The Bible tells us that Noah's sons, Shem, Ham, and Japheth, went on to become the ancestors of all the nations of the world, each developing their own unique cultures and knowledge.

The story of the Great Flood is a reminder of the importance of using wisdom responsibly. When people misuse their knowledge for evil purposes, it can lead to devastating consequences. The flood demonstrates God's desire for humanity to live righteously and follow His commandments. It also highlights the fragility of human knowledge and the need to preserve and pass down wisdom to future generations. By learning from the mistakes of the past, we can strive to build a better and more just world. The world before the flood was a place of great wisdom and knowledge, much of which was lost or erased during the flood. The Bible teaches us that this loss was a consequence of humanity's corruption and misuse of their gifts. By studying the story of the flood, we can appreciate the value of wisdom and the importance of living in accordance with God's will.

"Be strong and courageous. Do not be afraid; do not be discouraged, for the Lord your God will be with you wherever you go."

- Joshua 1:9 (NIV)

Long ago, in the ancient land of Assyria, a powerful battle was taking place. This battle happened in what we now call Ukraine. The warriors, known as Saxons or Norsemen, were the first horsemen of war. They rode their horses with great skill and bravery. These horsemen were very strong and fearless, and they scared their enemies with their fast and powerful attacks. Since the beginning, the Assyrians were known for being excellent fighters. The Saxons or Norsemen, with their long hair and fierce looks, were perfect examples of great cavalry warriors. They practiced a lot to ride their horses and fight at the same time. Their weapons, like spears and swords, were made very well, so they could hit their enemies accurately. During the battle, the horsemen used smart techniques. They would charge at their enemies in a tight group, making a loud noise with their horses' hooves. When they reached the enemy lines, they spread out and started fighting hand-to-hand. This way, they could break through the enemy's defenses and cause confusion. The Saxons were not only good riders but also strong fighters on the ground.

The Assyrian army saw how effective the horsemen were and decided to learn from them. They trained their soldiers to ride horses and fight just like the Saxons. This new way of fighting helped the Assyrians expand their empire and win more battles. The ancient battlefield in Assyria became a place where these new tactics were tested. These early horsemen became soon become the symbols of power and respect. People admired their skills and bravery. Stories and legends about their heroism were told and passed down through generations. These tales inspired future warriors to be just as excellent. The legacy of the Saxons or Norsemen lived on, influencing how cavalry tactics were developed in later civilizations.

Table of Contents

Chapter 1: The Forgotten Laws: Words That Rule the World

"Words are, in my not-so-humble opinion, our most inexhaustible source of magic."
– J.K. Rowling

Words are more than mere sounds or symbols scratched onto paper — they are the very instruments through which reality is shaped. Every civilization that has risen and fallen did so on the strength of its language. Words have built empires, sparked revolutions, written laws, and anchored spiritual beliefs. They are not just tools of communication but instruments of power, influence, and sometimes, manipulation. When a person speaks, they are not simply producing sound — they are casting intention into the world. Just as a builder uses bricks to construct a house, we use words to construct meaning, agreements, laws, and even identities.

Take, for instance, the phrase "I do." In a wedding ceremony, those two tiny words bind two lives together in the eyes of society and often under law. The phrase "You are guilty" can sentence a person to years behind bars. The words "We the People" laid the foundation of a nation's constitution. The words we choose — and the words chosen for us — carry weight, consequences, and sometimes, secrets.

But what happens when words mean one thing to the public and something entirely different in the legal world?

This is where the **dual nature of language** becomes evident — particularly in the legal system. Most of us grow up understanding language through everyday usage. We learn that "person" means a human being. We believe that "understanding" is about mental clarity. But in the world of law, these words may take on completely different — and sometimes deliberately deceptive — meanings. Take the term *person* for example. According to Black's Law Dictionary, a widely used legal reference, *person* can mean a legal entity such as a corporation, not necessarily a living human being. This linguistic sleight of hand creates a separation between our common sense understanding and the legal definition being applied to us.

In everyday life, we hear "submit" and think of turning in a paper or yielding in an argument. In court, however, "submit" can imply full agreement and acceptance of the court's jurisdiction. This subtle but powerful shift in definition can have far-reaching implications. Most people unknowingly enter legal contracts or accept terms and conditions that contain phrases with specialized meanings — meanings that are often hidden in plain sight. This is how language becomes a tool not only for justice but, at times, for silent control.

Legal systems across the world are built on foundations that the average citizen rarely questions. They rest on ancient legacies — systems of thought, governance, and spiritual authority that stretch back thousands of years. The very structure of modern law owes much to Roman civil law, canon law from religious institutions, and maritime or admiralty law, which governed trade and conduct at sea. These systems were heavily coded, not just in structure but in language. They were designed to be understood only by the initiated—the trained scribes, clerics, and judges—while the rest of the population remained unaware of the full scope of what the words and terms actually meant.

These **unseen forces**—the legacies of ancient language and hidden definitions—still shape our world today. When we walk into a courtroom, we often believe we are entering a place of fairness and transparency. But what we're often entering is a theater of rituals, a highly codified system where the words spoken and the words written can have drastically different implications. It is a realm where silence can mean consent, where standing at the wrong time can imply guilt, and where a simple nod can carry contractual weight.

To truly understand the world we live in, we must learn to **decode the language** that governs it. We must question the terms, research the definitions, and read between the lines. Because if we don't define our words, someone else will—and in doing so, they will define the terms of our lives.

Language, when understood deeply, becomes a doorway. It reveals the true nature of power structures, belief systems, and historical truths long buried beneath polite conversation and everyday phrases. It is time we began to see language not just as a tool, but as a map—one filled with ancient routes, hidden messages, and silent agreements that shape the world far more than we realize.

In examining the genealogical history, we encounter a significant distinction between the lineages of Ashkenaz and those of the Semitic tribes. Ashkenaz, as recorded in ancient texts, is said to descend from Japheth, the son of Noah. Meanwhile, the tribes of Israel trace their roots through Shem, another son of Noah. This differentiation suggests that Ashkenaz, according to traditional genealogies, is not part of the Semitic lineage, but rather from a different branch entirely.

Genesis 10:3 provides a glimpse into this ancient structure: "And the sons of Gomer: Ashkenaz, and Riphath, and Togarmah" (KJV 1611). This verse highlights the separation of Ashkenaz from the line that would later come to define the Jewish people as we know them. In modern discourse, we commonly associate the term "Semitic" with Arabic-speaking populations, yet it's worth considering how cultural identities evolve over time, particularly when confronted with historical shifts.

In fact, the term "Jewish" itself did not enter common use until well after a period of significant transformation. Historical records suggest that around the 8th century AD, certain groups, far from their ancient ancestral lands, adopted new religious practices. This process was marked by their eventual integration into a broader community that came to be recognized as part of the Jewish faith, even though their origins were not directly tied to the ancient tribes of Israel.

This shift in identity is a reminder of the complex and often invisible forces that shape cultural and religious affiliations over time. Just as language and history can reshape a people's destiny, so too can the interpretation of ancient genealogies inform our understanding of the past, even if the details remain clouded by time and circumstance.

As we peel back the layers of legal language and its hidden meanings, we begin to uncover not just a manipulation of words — but an entire **framework of control** embedded in our global systems. The story doesn't end with definitions from Black's Law Dictionary. It deepens with historical events and legal constructs that still shape our understanding of freedom, identity, and ownership today.

Consider the **Treaty of Paris** of 1783. It is celebrated as the moment the United States gained independence from Britain. However, few pause to read the fine print of the agreement itself. The treaty, signed by representatives of the Crown and the American colonies, did not declare complete severance. Instead, it emphasized the repayment of debts to British merchants, protected property of loyalists, and, crucially, maintained commercial and legal ties between the new nation and the British Empire. In other words, **the rights we think we won were not fully granted — they were conditionally reserved**.

This carefully crafted language reflects a broader theme: **power never simply disappears — it adapts, hides, and often embeds itself in legal terms and overlooked footnotes**. The Treaty of Paris serves as a prime example of how control can persist under the illusion of freedom. Independence was declared — but ownership and legal superiority, especially in commercial law, were never truly surrendered.

To understand how deeply this strategy of concealment runs, we must look at an even earlier event: **The Great Fire**

of London in 1666. While remembered as a catastrophic blaze that destroyed much of the city, it coincided with something even more transformative — the passage of the **Cestui Que Vie Act of 1666**. This law, passed quietly during the chaos, allowed the Crown to claim ownership over the property and legal identity of any individual who was considered "lost at sea" or otherwise presumed dead. With much of London in disarray and records destroyed, this legal move enabled the Crown to assume broad administrative and financial control over its subjects — without them even knowing it.

But this wasn't just about rebuilding a city. It was about redefining **identity** itself.

The term *Cestui Que Vie* (French for "he who lives") referred to a legal trust established to manage the estate or assets of someone believed to be dead. Under this doctrine, every individual was effectively treated as a legal fiction — a name on paper, not a living soul. When a child is born today, their birth certificate is issued and registered — not merely as a record of life, but as the creation of a **legal entity**. That entity, in many systems, is then used in financial markets as collateral. A human being becomes two things: a living soul and a corporate shell. One is real. The other is paper.

This legal fiction — **the "straw man" or legal person** — is a legacy of that 1666 trust framework. Most people live their entire lives unaware of the distinction between their living self and the legal version of themselves created at birth. The rights and restrictions that govern them often apply to the legal entity, not the human being. But if you do not know the difference, you operate under rules that were never meant to serve your freedom — they were crafted to manage property.

Thus, the language of law becomes a veil. It conceals the true nature of identity, power, and control under centuries of tradition, symbol, and ceremony. We're not simply participants in society — we are unknowingly actors on a stage, following scripts we did not write, governed by systems we did not choose.

And yet, knowledge is power. To understand how language and law have been used to create these hidden frameworks is to take the first step toward reclaiming personal sovereignty. When we begin to ask not just *what* the law says, but *who* it applies to — and in what capacity — we start to untangle the web spun so carefully through treaties, trusts, and terms.

The question we must ask is simple: **Are we living beings under divine law — or names under contract?**

In the chapters to come, we'll explore how these hidden codes extend far beyond identity, into commerce, education, religion, and governance. But for now, one truth stands clear: **words are not just symbols — they are spells.** And those who master the language, master the world.

Chapter 2: The World Before the Great Flood

"The farther backward you can look, the farther forward you are likely to see."
– Winston Churchill

Before the world we know was etched into stone tablets and scrolls, before the rise of Mesopotamia, Egypt, or the Indus Valley, there existed another world—an age now veiled in myth, suspicion, and fragmented memory. This was the Antediluvian Era: a time before the Great Flood. Modern science and ancient texts both whisper about this forgotten age, hinting at a sophisticated humanity whose knowledge, culture, and technology rival—if not surpass—our own.

Civilizations rose and fell long before the official story of history begins. The relics of their existence are scattered across the planet: cyclopean structures, submerged cities, and anomalous artifacts that defy explanation. These echoes from a pre-flood world offer a glimpse into the knowledge humanity once held—and then lost in cataclysm.

Younger Dryas Era: The Cataclysm That Reset History

Roughly 12,800 years ago, Earth underwent one of its most mysterious and devastating transitions: the **Younger Dryas**. Named after an Arctic flower that flourished during this sudden cooling period, the Younger Dryas marked a violent interruption in the planet's climate stability. Temperatures plunged globally within a matter of years. Ecosystems collapsed. Megafauna went extinct. But more importantly—**entire civilizations may have disappeared beneath the rising seas and falling ash.**

Scientific theories point to a possible cosmic trigger: a fragmented comet or asteroid impact that struck the Northern Hemisphere, sending debris and fire into the sky. This is supported by the discovery of a **black mat layer**—a thin strip of carbon-rich sediment found across multiple continents, filled with nanodiamonds and microspherules typically associated with high-heat impact events. What followed was a mini ice age, melting ice caps, and rising oceans that may have submerged entire cultures and cities.

Ancient texts echo these events. The Epic of Gilgamesh, the Sumerian King List, the Bible's Genesis, and Hindu scriptures like the Mahabharata all speak of a great flood—a divine reset triggered not only by divine judgment but by environmental cataclysm. The striking similarity in global flood narratives suggests that the Younger Dryas was not just a geological event—it was **a civilizational extinction**. A deliberate reset or an uncontrollable purge? That answer remains buried.

Evidence from Japan and India – Who Were the Forgotten Builders?

In modern academia, history is supposed to begin around 5,000 years ago with the emergence of writing. But **what if that timeline is missing entire chapters?** Underwater discoveries in Japan and India suggest precisely that.

In **Yonaguni, Japan**, off the southern coast of Okinawa, lies a submerged megalithic structure that defies conventional explanation. Massive stone terraces, staircases, and platforms rise from the seabed—too geometrically precise to be purely natural formations. Some archaeologists claim they are natural rock formations shaped by tectonic activity. But others argue they were carved—by human hands—before the last Ice Age ended. If true, that would place their construction **at least 10,000**

years ago, long before the rise of Egyptian or Sumerian architecture.

In **the Gulf of Khambhat (Cambay), India**, sonar imaging in 2001 revealed ruins beneath 120 feet of water—grids of what appear to be streets, foundations, and walls. Carbon-dated artifacts retrieved from the site suggest a civilization over 9,000 years old. For reference, this predates the Harappan Civilization by several millennia. Skeptics argue over dating methods and provenance of artifacts, but the implications are profound: **Who built these cities, and why did they disappear?**

These submerged sites suggest the presence of highly organized, technologically advanced societies capable of urban planning, architecture, and possibly navigation. They hint at a **pre-flood civilization** that may have rivaled our own—until it was swallowed by the sea.

What Knowledge Was Buried Beneath the Flood?

Knowledge, like light, illuminates everything it touches. But when a flood comes, both can be extinguished in an instant. The deluge—whether mythological or geological—was not just an erasure of people. It was an erasure of **memory**. Libraries drowned. Oral traditions cut short. Machines rusted into oblivion. The survivors had only fragments—and with those fragments, they began again.

What did we lose?

We may never know the full answer, but clues survive in the myths and megaliths. Ancient stories from Egypt, India, Sumeria, and even Mesoamerica tell of **gods or sages** who once walked among humans—beings of immense knowledge who taught agriculture, astronomy, medicine, architecture, and law. These "gods" may not have been divine at all, but remnants of an earlier people who survived the cataclysm and tried to pass on what they knew.

Some researchers believe that **sacred geometry**, advanced astronomical alignments, and even certain linguistic structures are echoes of Antediluvian wisdom. Sites like Gobekli Tepe—dated to at least 11,000 years ago—show not just primitive carvings but symbolic sophistication. Why build a megalithic temple with perfect celestial alignment if your culture is supposedly pre-agricultural?

Could it be that what we call **"ancient knowledge"** is merely **post-flood memory**—fragments preserved by survivors? Knowledge of sound, vibration, sacred mathematics, herbal medicine, natural law, and cosmic cycles? Perhaps the stories of Atlantis, Lemuria, or Mu are not mere fantasy—but distorted memories of real civilizations that once flourished, then vanished beneath the waters.

The flood did more than drown cities—it drowned **a paradigm**. A way of thinking, building, healing, and living that we can only reconstruct through myth, stone, and intuition. And maybe, just maybe, the return of that knowledge lies not in discovering something new—but in **remembering what we once knew.**

Nearly every ancient civilization—from the Mesopotamians and Hebrews to the Hopi, Mayans, and Sumerians—shares a story of a great flood. These tales stretch across time and geography, embedded deep within sacred texts, oral traditions, and carved stone. Despite vast cultural differences, the essence remains strangely consistent: humanity had grown corrupt or prideful, and a cataclysmic deluge swept the world clean. Survivors—often warned by a divine force—preserved life and knowledge, starting anew in a reformed world. This recurring pattern begs the question: how could so many unrelated societies conceive of the same myth unless it stemmed from a shared truth? The universality of the flood narrative suggests more than mere coincidence. It points to a global memory, encoded in myth, of an event—or series of events—so traumatic and transformative that it left an indelible imprint on the human psyche.

The Abrahamic version, told in Genesis, frames the flood as a divine judgment: a correction, not of climate, but of character. In this telling, the earth was "filled with violence," and the Creator resolved to undo what had gone astray. Noah, righteous among men, was chosen to preserve a remnant—his family and pairs of every creature. The language of the text is clear: this was not a symbolic flood, but a total, world-consuming reset. Some interpret it spiritually, as a metaphor for the purging of sin. Others argue it speaks to an actual historical purge—one veiled in religious imagery but rooted in real events, such as the Younger Dryas cataclysm or massive post-glacial floods. If the Abrahamic flood was a divine reset, was it meant to cleanse the earth of violence alone—or also knowledge deemed too dangerous to preserve? Some traditions whisper that it wasn't just humanity that was lost in the flood, but also wisdom—about the heavens, the earth, and the laws that govern both.

After the flood, the story doesn't slow—it escalates. Humanity, repopulated through Noah's descendants, unites once again. They share a single language and a common ambition: to reach the heavens. Thus, they begin to build a tower—tall enough to defy the boundaries between mortal and divine. The Tower of Babel, often dismissed as legend, holds profound implications. It reveals the fear of centralized power, of human beings achieving too much unity, knowledge, or advancement. According to the biblical account, God intervened—not by destroying the structure, but by shattering the unity. Language was confounded, and people were scattered across the earth. It was not a punishment of destruction, but of division. A global society fractured by speech, no longer able to coordinate, progress, or perhaps, rebel. This linguistic scattering wasn't just about communication—it was about control. It suggests a deeper lesson: when humanity speaks with one voice, it becomes powerful enough to challenge even the divine. But divided by tongues, it forgets its shared origin and instead becomes easier to rule.

Taken together, the stories of the flood and the tower reflect a pattern of erasure followed by confusion. First, the slate is wiped clean. Then, the surviving remnants are divided and distracted. Whether by divine design, historical purge, or orchestrated cover-up, the result is the same: a break in the transmission of knowledge. A rupture in collective memory. And a world that begins again—but forgets where it started. The past becomes myth. The truth becomes taboo. And those who question too deeply are told not to build towers, nor to look for what lies beneath the floodwaters. But perhaps the deeper lesson is not in the punishment, but in the remembering. What we lost. Why we lost it. And what we must reclaim before history repeats itself again.

Chapter 3: The Rise of Nations: Control, Culture, and Belief

"History is written by the victors—but civilization is rebuilt by the survivors."
– Anonymous

After the waters receded and the echoes of the flood faded into memory, the world entered a new era. A blank slate had been forced upon humanity. The survivors, whether Noah's descendants, ancient kings, or scattered tribal leaders, faced the task of rebuilding—not just homes and farms, but societies. With the loss of countless lives came the loss of languages, records, structures, and most tragically, knowledge. What emerged in the aftermath were civilizations that bore the scars of memory and myth—societies that sought meaning in what they had survived and that leaned on new systems of belief to explain the forces that had both destroyed and spared them. From this broken soil, **new cultures rose**, seeded by those who remembered fragments of the old world but had to forge a new one by necessity.

Belief systems became central to this reconstruction. Some viewed the flood as divine punishment, others as a cosmic reset. Either way, the spiritual interpretation of the event shaped the moral and legal codes of emerging societies. Religion took center stage, not just as a path to salvation or enlightenment, but as a **guiding structure for order**. In Mesopotamia, Egypt, India, and later in Greece and Rome, spiritual belief became the scaffold on which governments were built. Gods were invoked to bless rulers; divine favor became the justification for law. But as civilizations expanded and power centralized, religion evolved from sacred mystery into something else entirely: a **tool**

for administration, a **lens for control**, and in many cases, a **means of limiting freedom rather than promoting it**.

Priesthoods became political classes. Temples became banks. Tithes became taxes. The line between spiritual and civic life blurred, until questioning one meant threatening both. The idea of divine right—where rulers were chosen by gods or were gods themselves—cemented the hierarchy. The masses were led to believe their station in life was ordained, unchangeable, and sacred. Thus, faith was transformed from a personal search for meaning into a tool for obedience. While spiritual truths may have remained intact for the initiated few, for the common people, religion often became **a filter through which all understanding was approved or denied**.

Yet out of this long history of centralized power—first in the name of gods, then kings, then empires—another experiment emerged. One that claimed to break the cycle. That experiment was **America**.

From its inception, the founding of the United States was positioned as a bold rejection of monarchy, feudalism, and imperial law. Its architects spoke of liberty, natural rights, and self-governance. But beneath the language of freedom and justice lay a **deliberate legal framework**, carefully chosen, that pulled threads from ancient Rome, biblical codes, and maritime law. The Founding Fathers, though often viewed through the lens of idealism, were not naive visionaries—they were legal tacticians. The Constitution, with its precise language, created a **system of governance bound tightly to the rule of law**—a law that could be interpreted, amended, or weaponized depending on who held the pen.

What made America unique was not just its break from monarchy, but its **institutionalization of control through lawful appearance**. It gave the illusion of consent through voting, of freedom through rights, and of sovereignty through citizenship. But in reality, America became **a new iteration of empire**—one based not on crowns or crosses, but on contracts. The law, rather than religion, became the new pulpit. Courts became the new temples. And lawyers replaced priests as interpreters of the sacred texts of governance.

Slavery was codified in the early documents. Land was taken under legal pretenses. Indigenous nations were written out of existence through treaties never honored. The legal language that built America also buried truths beneath it—truths about who was free, who was counted, and who was ever truly sovereign. The Constitution promised liberty, but only to those recognized by the system as persons—a term, as discussed before, that carries dual meanings in legal contexts.

The rebuilding of society after the flood was not a simple act of survival. It was an act of **redefinition**—of values, of power, of identity. Whether guided by genuine spirituality or manipulated by legal codes, the reconstruction of the world created new paradigms. Those who understood the structures shaped them. Those who did not—lived within them.

And so, we return to the fundamental question: Are we the inheritors of a world rebuilt for liberty—or for silent obedience? The evidence suggests a mix of both. The challenge before us is not to tear down what has been built, but to uncover what lies beneath it—and to choose, with full knowledge, whether to live by inherited systems or to author new ones. Because every civilization is rebuilt, not by accident, but by intention. And in that intention, we find either our freedom—or our chains.

Beneath the surface of governments and rituals, beyond the parchment of laws and scriptures, an invisible war has been unfolding for millennia. It is not a war of armies or borders, but of worldviews—a struggle between the soul's yearning for liberation and the systems built to contain it. Spirituality, in its purest form, is about seeking truth, transcending boundaries, and remembering one's connection to the divine. But as civilizations grew and authority became centralized, this inner journey increasingly clashed with the outer world's demand for order, obedience, and conformity. What began as a sacred exploration of self became, in many places, an institutionalized path—guarded not by mystics, but by laws and dogma.

Few examples illustrate this collision better than the strange overlap between judiciary systems and ancient practices like necromancy. On the surface, one represents law and order; the other, an arcane art used to communicate with spirits of the dead. But examine them more closely and the parallels grow unsettling. In necromancy, the practitioner summons a spirit into a space and binds it to answer questions, often through a ritual. In courtrooms, a person is summoned—often unknowingly as a legal entity, a "person" on paper—then bound to legal jurisdiction through verbal and behavioral cues. The black robes of judges, the structured rituals, the invocation of oaths, and the invocation of a "dead" legal identity mirror spiritual rites more than civic arbitration. It's as though the legal system was designed as a secular priesthood, with its own incantations, symbols, and consequences. A world where the law doesn't just govern behavior—but seeks dominion over the very soul.

Within the Abrahamic religions—Judaism, Christianity, and Islam—this tension is even more visible. All three began with deep mystical roots: direct encounters with God, inner transformation, and an emphasis on compassion, justice, and humility. But over time, these faiths were shaped by empires and molded by institutions. Rules were formalized. Scriptures were canonized. Hierarchies were established. What was once a **path to divine union** became, in many cases, a **system for defining who was worthy and who was not**. The soul's journey was outsourced to clerics. Questioning became heresy. And obedience became the chief virtue.

This is not to say that Abrahamic faiths are inherently limiting—at their core, they still carry immense wisdom, beauty, and transformative power. But the way they have been administered by religious authorities and co-opted by political powers has often steered them away from personal awakening and toward institutional control. When a sacred path is reduced to a checklist of rituals or laws, the seeker is discouraged from exploring deeper truths. The result is a religion that serves the state, rather than a spirituality that frees the soul.

This transformation is part of a broader shift in human values—**from curiosity to obedience**. Early civilizations revered those who asked questions, who pushed boundaries, who communed with nature and the unseen. Shamans, philosophers, seers, and sages were once the pillars of wisdom. But as empires solidified and laws were etched into stone, curiosity became dangerous. Those who asked too many questions threatened the stability of the system. Obedience was elevated as a virtue, curiosity downgraded to rebellion. The message was clear: do not look beyond what we have given you.

This inversion of values can still be seen today in education systems that prioritize memorization over inquiry, in religious settings that discourage dialogue, and in governments that promote security over freedom. The invisible war is not fought with swords or guns—it is fought with definitions, with language, with fear. It is a war for the right to think, to question, to know.

And yet, the soul does not forget. Beneath the layers of law and ritual, something ancient stirs—a memory of freedom, of communion, of inner knowing. The invisible war may be old, but it is not over. Every time someone questions the meaning behind a law, a phrase, a religious rule, or a societal norm, they join the resistance. They step outside the prescribed story and begin to write their own.

In this war, victory is not about destroying the system—it is about remembering who you are within it. And once remembered, you cannot be controlled. Because no law, no doctrine, no judge or priest can own a soul that knows it is already free.

Chapter 4: The Battle Between Spirituality and Control

"The most potent weapon in the hands of the oppressor is the mind of the oppressed."
– Steve Biko

There has been a persistent and quiet war against spiritual awakening for as long as systems of power have existed. Enlightenment—true, inner realization of one's divine nature—has always posed a threat to any structure built on obedience. The awakened human is not easily governed. They ask questions. They follow conscience over command. They recognize the difference between the sacred and the counterfeit. And for centuries, those in positions of religious, legal, and political authority have understood this threat. Which is why, time and time again, enlightenment has been hidden, twisted, or outright criminalized.

In ancient cultures, the spiritual seeker was often revered. But as societies became empires, and empires needed uniformity, spirituality was slowly institutionalized. Mystics were replaced by theologians. Experience was replaced by doctrine. Revelation was replaced by law. The inward journey—the one that leads to self-realization and spiritual sovereignty—became inaccessible to most. The masses were given ceremonies, commandments, and creeds, but told not to look beyond them. To awaken fully meant to see beyond the veil. And those who could see— Socrates, Jesus, Hypatia, Giordano Bruno, Galileo—were often ridiculed, imprisoned, or killed. The lesson was clear: **do not seek beyond what you are told is truth.**

Over time, humanity has not just been discouraged from awakening—we have been **domesticated**. Conditioned, like animals in a pen, to follow paths laid before us. From birth, we are given names, numbers, and paperwork. We are educated in systems that reward conformity. We are taught what to think, not how to think. We are sold stories about success and survival, while our inner compass—the one tuned to freedom—is dulled. The domestication is not through chains or cages, but through **expectations, language, and fear**. Free will, the greatest gift given to humanity, has become the most tightly managed resource on Earth.

This silent war doesn't come with declarations or armies. It comes through systems that present themselves as protectors. Legal institutions claim to guard our rights. But many of them are built on frameworks that **presume ownership**, not guardianship. This is where necromancy and the law intersect again—in ways most never see.

The term "necromancy" once referred solely to the practice of communicating with the dead. But what happens when the legal system itself begins treating the living as if they were dead? Consider the birth certificate. When a child is born, a certificate is issued—documenting their arrival. But in legal terms, that certificate doesn't recognize a soul. It creates a **legal entity**—a "person" in the eyes of the state. A fiction. A corporate shell. And unless a living man or woman takes explicit steps to separate themselves from this entity, they are treated, in many legal systems, as if they are operating under **presumed incapacity**. Like a vessel adrift at sea. Lost. Legally absent.

Enter the role of the Attorney General—a title that carries more spiritual weight than most realize. "General" is a military term. "Attorney" is one who acts in place of another. This official oversees not merely justice, but **estate law**—the legal handling of trusts, titles, and, crucially, the estates of the presumed dead. If you have not proven your status as alive in the legal sense, you are considered administratively deceased. The certificate of aliveness—also called an affidavit of living status—is one of the few ways a man or woman can declare their consciousness, sovereignty, and refusal to be treated as a dead entity in the legal fiction. It is, quite literally, **a statement that you are not a ghost in the machine.**

Why does such a certificate exist at all? Why must a living being declare themselves as such to the very system that birthed them? The answer is unsettling: because the system was never built to honor your life—it was built to **manage your estate**. The fiction of the "person" is easier to tax, easier to fine, easier to control. The living man or woman is a wild variable—unpredictable, free, and dangerous to the carefully coded rules of governance.

This is the war that few recognize. A war not of violence, but of **definition**. A war that replaces spirit with paper, curiosity with compliance, and living truth with dead letters. And yet, awakening is still possible. Because despite all attempts to domesticate, suppress, and rewrite us—we are still here. Still alive. And when a soul remembers its origin, no law, no document, no courtroom in the world can contain it.

To awaken is not merely to know. It is to *remember*. To rise from the administrative dead. To reclaim what was quietly taken: not just your body or your name, but your **will**, your **path**, your **light**. And in doing so, you do not just escape the system. You outgrow it.

Reality, for most, is a passive backdrop—a stage upon which life plays out. We're taught to believe in a physical world made up of fixed laws, solid matter, and linear time. But ancient wisdom, modern physics, and direct spiritual experience all suggest something far more mysterious: **reality is not static—it is participatory**. It responds to awareness. It molds itself around attention. It is not simply observed—it observes back.

This isn't abstract mysticism—it's deeply embedded in the structure of the universe. Quantum mechanics reveals that particles do not settle into a specific state unless they are observed. The act of measurement changes the outcome. The observer influences the observed. At the smallest, most fundamental level, the universe is not made of matter—it is made of possibility. And what causes one possibility to manifest over another? **Consciousness.** Awareness. You.

This turns the familiar notion of reality on its head. We are not wandering through a world already decided. We are part of its unfolding—each thought, belief, and emotion helping to sculpt the experience we call life. Reality is **alive**, in dialogue with us. It is not just a place—it is a mirror, a collaborator, and in some profound sense, **a witness**.

Creation, as we understand it, appears to exist within time. Things have a beginning, middle, and end. The clock ticks. The sun rises and sets. But beneath the illusion of linearity lies something eternal. **Creation did not happen once—it is always happening.** Time is a structure built for the experience of change, not the source of creation itself. From the perspective of the eternal, all things exist at once. Past, present, and future are not events—but dimensions. We live in time, yes—but **we are not bound by it**. We come from something timeless. Our souls know this, even when our minds forget.

The ancients understood this. They encoded truths not in formulas, but in **symbols**—shapes, creatures, and parables designed to transmit knowledge across generations. One such forgotten symbol is the **bug and the belly**. At first glance, this pairing seems arbitrary—insignificant even. But there is hidden meaning here, one that speaks to the forgotten mechanics of reality.

The **bug** has long been a metaphor for consciousness. Small, often overlooked, yet capable of great instinct and awareness. In many cultures, insects symbolize transformation, adaptability, and a connection to the invisible world. The scarab beetle in Egypt represented the eternal cycle of life and death. The butterfly in Native lore symbolized the soul's journey. Bugs are everywhere—quiet witnesses to reality's undercurrents.

The **belly**, meanwhile, represents creation. The womb of reality. The place where ideas, life, and emotions are nurtured into being. In Eastern traditions, the belly is the seat of the second brain— the gut feeling, the intuitive knowing. It is where we digest not only food but experience, memory, and meaning. The belly is the bridge between the formless and the formed.

Together, **bug and belly** tell a hidden story. Consciousness (bug) and manifestation (belly) are not separate—they are one process. Awareness begets creation. What we focus on in our gut—in our instinct, our imagination, our emotional truth—becomes real. The forgotten truth is that reality does not come at us from the outside—it flows through us, from the inside out.

And here lies the greatest illusion of all: that we are passive residents in a predetermined world. In truth, we are **participants in an ongoing act of creation**. We are not just being watched— we are doing the watching. We are not just shaped—we are shaping.

So who is watching? You are. And the deeper part of you—the part that is eternal, free from name or time—is doing more than watching. It is dreaming this reality into form. What you call the world is not out there. It is happening **through you**. The bug and the belly remind us: the smallest spark of awareness contains the whole flame. And when you remember this, the nature of reality changes—not because the world changes, but because **you do**.

Chapter 5: The Individual vs. The System

"Before we learn the world, we *are* the world—entire, aware, and one with all that is."
– Anonymous

Long before we speak, before we walk, before we understand our own name, we *know*. Not through facts or logic, but through something more ancient—spiritual intuition. The kind of knowing that precedes language, culture, and belief systems. It is the knowing of presence. Of being.

The Babylonian Talmud—a sacred text of Jewish oral tradition—makes an extraordinary claim: that infants are more spiritual than adults. According to the tradition, every child in the womb is taught all the wisdom of the universe. They are shown the entire Torah, the hidden mysteries, and the fabric of divine knowledge. And then, just before birth, an angel touches the infant above the lip, causing them to forget. That sacred touch—the indentation we all carry between nose and mouth— is called the "philtrum." It is a symbolic reminder of the wisdom we once held, and the forgetting that follows birth.

This mystical idea carries profound spiritual implications. It suggests that we *begin* with knowledge—not ignorance. That consciousness doesn't gradually awaken, but is dimmed, filtered, and constrained by the process of growing into the world. In this view, babies are not blank slates. They are closer to Source. They are still radiant with the light of where they came from— unburdened by constructs, untouched by dogma, unstained by fear.

This is not just spiritual poetry. It reflects something many parents, midwives, and sensitive observers know intuitively: infants often seem aware of more than what meets the eye. They gaze into corners where no one stands. They smile at seemingly nothing. Their cries are not always rooted in pain or need, but in something unseen—perhaps a longing for the place they came from. The mystery of birth is not merely biological; it is spiritual migration—from the eternal into the temporal, from soul into body.

Modern science struggles to explain these early perceptions, often dismissing them as developmental randomness. But indigenous wisdom across cultures—from the Maori to the Navajo to African cosmologies—affirms that babies are still "in-between worlds." Their consciousness, still soft and open, can perceive what adults have long tuned out. In their eyes, we sometimes see something vast—something remembering.

But what happens next is predictable, even tragic: *we teach them otherwise.*

With time, the child is named, numbered, and labeled. They are taught to see the world through filters—language, logic, hierarchy, fear. We replace intuition with instruction. We silence inner voices with external authority. Slowly, the veil descends. The child forgets who they are and begins to learn who they are *supposed* to be. Thus begins the domestication of the soul.

This process is not malicious. It is cultural. Systemic. Generational. But it comes at a cost: the first knowledge—the primal spiritual awareness—is lost beneath layers of conditioning. The child who once remembered the stars begins to fear the dark. The one who spoke with the unseen becomes skeptical of what cannot be measured. And the being who was once whole becomes a citizen, a student, a subject.

Yet that original knowledge—the pure, quiet knowing—is not gone. It is merely buried. It remains within us, beneath the noise of thought, the weight of identity, and the noise of civilization. Some call it intuition. Others call it soul memory. It's the reason we sometimes cry without knowing why. The reason déjà vu shakes us. The reason music can move us to tears. These are echoes of a knowing we did not learn—we brought it with us.

To remember this is to awaken. And awakening, as always, begins not by adding more—but by removing. Peeling back the layers of what we've been taught, until we return to what we've always known.

Beneath every empire, behind every law, beyond every cultural norm, there are forces—silent, unnamed, but deeply effective. They do not announce themselves in speeches or headlines. They do not wear crowns or wave flags. They move invisibly—through habits, traditions, products, phrases, symbols. And yet, they shape the very structure of how we think, feel, and live. The question is not whether they exist—but whether we dare to see them.

Courage vs. Silence: What History Teaches Us About Obedience

In every era, there have been those who saw the veil—and those who lifted it. But more often, there were those who did not. Not because they were blind, but because they were afraid. History is not merely a chronicle of battles and empires—it is a record of obedience and its consequences. What separates the free from the captive, the enlightened from the subdued, is rarely knowledge alone. It is the courage to speak.

In Nazi Germany, millions remained silent—not because they agreed, but because they feared becoming targets. In Stalin's Russia, entire families whispered their truths in kitchens, terrified of the knock at the door. In colonial regimes across

Africa, Asia, and the Americas, those who questioned authority were branded "rebels," while those who complied were given titles, jobs, and just enough illusion of safety. Obedience became the currency of survival. But silence is not neutral. It is not simply the absence of noise. It is a choice—a response to fear, or worse, indifference.

And yet, courage is not loud. It does not always roar. Sometimes it is the small voice that says "no" when everyone else nods. It is the refusal to conform when conformity is the path to reward. It is the ancient soul memory that knows truth is not negotiable, even when it is inconvenient. Every generation is offered a test: obey for comfort, or speak for freedom. Most choose the former. But history remembers the latter.

Those who stayed silent during injustice believed they were preserving peace. But what they preserved was the system. The control. The lie. Real peace never requires silence—it requires truth. And truth always comes at a cost.

The Turmeric–Slavery Connection: Hidden Ties to Power and Control

It may seem strange—almost absurd—to mention turmeric and slavery in the same breath. One is a kitchen spice, praised for its color and healing. The other, a human atrocity that spanned continents. But this juxtaposition is not random. It is a key to understanding how the unspoken forces of control often hide in plain sight.

Turmeric, a golden root revered in Ayurvedic medicine and Eastern spirituality, has long symbolized purification, health, and sacred ritual. In Indian households, it was not just an ingredient—it was a healing presence. A protector. A spiritual ally. But when colonial powers arrived in India, they did not simply conquer land—they commodified knowledge. Ancient traditions were stripped of meaning and reduced to exports.

Spices like turmeric became goods—devoid of their sacred context, harvested for profit.

This commodification mirrored what was happening elsewhere: human beings were also reduced to units of labor. The transatlantic slave trade turned souls into property. People were shipped like cargo. Like spices. The same colonial empires that praised turmeric in European apothecaries were, at the same time, trafficking human lives from Africa. Both were used—one to flavor, the other to build. Both were valued for what they could produce, not for what they were.

Even today, turmeric is marketed as a "superfood"—a trendy wellness item divorced from its spiritual origins. Most consumers are unaware that turmeric's global spread was fueled not just by trade, but by domination. It moved through the same colonial arteries that trafficked bodies, lands, and traditions. The sacred was turned into commerce. The spiritual became the commercial.

This is how unspoken forces operate. Not through war—but through repackaging. They take what is holy and make it profitable. They erase the story, but keep the symbol. And in doing so, they control the narrative of culture, memory, and meaning.

To reclaim our sovereignty, we must begin to see these connections—not as isolated facts, but as patterns. Patterns of power. The turmeric in your kitchen. The silence in your family. The courage you were taught to suppress. These are not unrelated threads. They are parts of the same tapestry—a tapestry woven by unseen hands for centuries.

But to see the tapestry is to begin unweaving it. Not with rage, but with awareness. Not to destroy—but to remember. To re-sanctify what was profaned. To give voice to what was silenced.

And to stand, once again, in the truth that has always been waiting beneath the surface.

* 9 7 9 8 8 9 3 9 7 7 6 2 2 *